How on earth did I end up here? I was supposed to be at a party kissing the boy of my dreams, instead I'm dancing naked on the town common, on Halloween, with a Coven of strange women who might be witches, a bunch of zombies that I have to return to their graves, a talking crow, and my house ghost thrown in for good measure. Just yesterday I was an ordinary teenager…

On her sixteenth birthday Emily Rand discovers that she is a witch. Unable to control her spells she unwittingly raises zombies, and corporealizes the ghost haunting her house. She finds herself in a race against time to put everything right if she has any hope of getting to a certain Halloween party and seeing a certain boy again.

## Books by Stella Wilkinson

The Flirting Games
More Flirting Games
Further Flirting Games
The Flirting Games Trilogy
Good @ Games
Flirting with Friends

Halloween Magic & Mayhem
Werewolf Magic & Mayhem
Solstice Magic & Mayhem

Romancing the Stove
Bend it like a Bookworm
Game, Set, and Mismatch

Notice Me
A Christmas Gift
All Hallows EVE

If you would like to be informed immediately when future books by this author are released then please sign up to the mailing list at: http://eepurl.com/wEMmD or visit the website www.stellawilkinson.com

Copyright © Stella Wilkinson 2014

All characters herein are fictitious and any resemblance to real persons, living or dead, is purely coincidental. All rights reserved. This book or any portion thereof may not be reproduced or used in any manner without the express written permission of the publisher or author except for the use of brief quotations in a book review.

**This book was written, produced and edited in the UK, where some spelling, grammar and word usage will vary from US English**

# Halloween Magic & Mayhem

## By
## Stella Wilkinson

Mum
Thank you
I couldn't have done it without you!

# Contents

Chapter One .................................................................... - 1 -

Chapter Two .................................................................. - 11 -

Chapter Three ............................................................... - 19 -

Chapter Four ................................................................. - 33 -

Chapter Five .................................................................. - 45 -

Chapter Six .................................................................... - 56 -

Chapter Seven ............................................................... - 71 -

## Chapter One

How on earth did I end up here? I was supposed to be at a party kissing the boy of my dreams, instead I'm dancing naked on the town common, on Halloween, with a Coven of strange women who might be witches, a bunch of zombies that I have to return to their graves, a talking crow, and my pet ghost thrown in for good measure. Just yesterday I was an ordinary teenager…

*One day earlier…*

I left school on Friday, thrilled to be free for the weekend. My best friends, Bryony and Kate, were discussing what costumes to wear to Tamsin Warner's Halloween party tomorrow night, and I was super excited too.

Tamsin seemed to have invited everyone in our year, as well as a few kids from the other school in town, one of whom was Sean Carrey.

Sean Carrey is the boy I like.

I had been in the local shopping centre a few weeks ago with my mates, when a bunch of boys started showing off in front of us on their skateboards. One, in particular, had caught my attention. He had brown hair with a floppy fringe that he kept flicking off his face, big brown eyes, and a dazzling smile. He knew he was cute. What had amazed me most about him was that he seemed to think I was cute too. Despite my being surrounded by some quite pretty female friends, he kept smiling at me. *Me*, plain, boring Emily Rand.

The only interesting thing about me is maybe my hair. It's long and dark. But my eyes are dishwater grey, I think my lips are too thin and my nose is too big. My dad keeps telling me I'm going to be "a great beauty some day", just like my mother was, but I think that day is quite a long way off right now. Plus, my dad is biased.

Anyway, this boy kept looking over, and my friends all noticed and started nudging me. I was embarrassed but secretly delighted.

Despite being nearly sixteen I haven't had much attention from boys, and this one was perfect for my first serious crush. He didn't go to our school, which was a major plus point. I've known all the boys in my school since we were five and clearly remember the phase where they all thought it was hilariously funny to wipe snot on my back; not to mention that time I spent the night at Kate's house and my spare knickers fell out of my bag onto the classroom floor and all the boys threw them back and forth whilst I howled in the toilets and refused to come out for three hours.

This boy had not been part of any of that; he was a mystery, without any childish past, and did I mention he was cute?

After about twenty minutes of showing off in front of us, his friends got chatting to my friends, and so naturally we talked a bit.

His name was Sean Carrey, he went to Fairgreen School on the other side of town, he was sixteen, and he liked pizza and he loved the Alien movies. That was about all I learned. Then his mates wanted to push off and he didn't ask for my number or anything, he just said, "See you around, Emily."

But I never did see him around.

I kept hoping to run into him again, despite being really nervous about doing so. I made my friends go back to the shopping centre every Saturday after, but we never found them.

Then last Monday Tamsin invited us to her party, and she mentioned that some of her friends were coming from Fairgreen. I didn't want to ask her about Sean, but I didn't have to; it turned out he had already asked Tamsin about me.

She was almost green with envy as she told me that Sean had specifically asked her if I was going to be there.

I blushed a lot, but it was a happy blush. He had remembered my name, *and* he told Tamsin to tell me that he was looking forward to seeing me at the party.

I was terrified that he might not really actually like me, and just as terrified that he might. I had no idea how to talk to a boy I liked. Was I supposed to flirt with him and pretend to be confident? It was far more likely I would sit in a corner and hope he'd come and talk to me. I just prayed I wouldn't completely humiliate myself by being totally unable to say anything remotely intelligent.

But it didn't matter, the important thing was that at long last there was a boy who liked me, and I was going to see him at the party.

I did a private happy dance when I got home, and then rushed to ask my dad if we could forget about my big birthday dinner.

Halloween is also my birthday, and this year is my Sweet Sixteen. Dad was going to lay on a "family dinner", which was nice of him but I don't actually like my so-called family.

By that I mean my dad's girlfriend and her son.

My mum died when I was five. I don't remember her that much, but it meant my dad and I were pretty close as I was growing up. So you can imagine how much I resented it when he starting to date again two years ago. Not only did his new girlfriend move into our house, but she brought her son with her: an immature pain in the bum called Duncan, who is only six months younger than me and is now in my class at school.

Dad's forever telling me I have to make sure Duncan's included in stuff I do out of school, but I hate having him follow me around, and I was relieved when he found his own group of idiots to hang with. Unfortunately it seemed they were also invited to the party.

Dad was disappointed about the family dinner but understood that I would rather go to a party.

"Maybe we can all get together beforehand and then you kids could go out after?" he suggested.

Personally I had intended to spend most of the early evening getting ready for the party, so I came up with an alternative.

"How about we have the family dinner on Sunday night instead? That way I can celebrate my sixteenth two nights running." I gave him an enthusiastic smile and he agreed, actually believing I wanted the family dinner. So we were all happy.

"By the way," he'd added, "your aunt called and said to remind you to go see her after school on Friday. She's invited you to stay for dinner. She said to tell you not to forget."

So school was finally over for the week, we had a party to look forward to tomorrow night, Sean Carrey was going to be there, and I was hoping for some decent money from my relatives for my sixteenth. Everything seemed good with the world.

I separated from Bryony and Kate at the corner of Milton Place and went to see my Aunt Iris.

Everyone in town knows Iris is a witch. Not the kind that rides around on a broomstick in a black hat, but the kind that burns incense and wears a lot of pagan jewellery. She doesn't make any secret of being a witch. In fact, she says it's good for business. She runs one of those shops that sells a lot of witchy paraphernalia. Books, coloured candles, silver pentagrams and crystal balls, all that sort of stuff.

Iris is my mother's sister, the only family I have left on that side, so we're pretty close. I'd secretly always hoped that she and my dad would fall in love, but they don't really get on. Mainly because of the witch thing, I think.

The bell tinkled over the door as I entered her shop and her cat, Lyra, jumped down off the windowsill to greet me. Lyra is generally quite unfriendly to most people, but she loves me, and twined around my legs purring hello.

I bent to stroke her, enjoying the dim light of the shop and its wonderful smells.

Iris came round from behind the counter and gave me a warm hug.

"Thank the goddess you're here at last," she said.

"I only finished school twenty minutes ago."

"I know, I'm just eager to see you." She walked over to the door and flipped the sign from Open to Closed, then locked the door.

"Aren't you supposed to be open until five?" I asked, confused.

She nodded. "Yes, but it's a quiet day, and you and I really need to talk undisturbed."

"That sounds ominous," I said in surprise.

She gave a strained laugh. "It's not 'ominous', no, but it is important."

We went upstairs to the flat she lived in over the shop.

Considering how important whatever it was she wanted to talk about apparently was, she took a very long time to get to the point. First we sat out on her roof terrace and drank nettle tea, while she asked me a bunch of questions about school. Then, when it got too cold, we went inside and carved pumpkins together while she told me lots of spooky Halloween stories. It wasn't until she'd made dinner and we sat down at her old oak table that she cleared her throat and said she had something to tell me.

I twirled spaghetti around my fork and tried to look interested, even though I was actually focusing on not getting tomato sauce on my clothes.

"You're sixteen tonight," she said, a bit

overdramatically.

"No," I corrected her, "my birthday is tomorrow. You know that."

She shook her head, "You officially turn sixteen tonight at midnight. There are things you should know before it happens."

"If this is about sex, then Dad already gave me *the talk*; it was embarrassing enough the first time, please don't make me sit through it again!" I begged her.

She laughed, "It's not about sex."

"Well, that's a relief anyway. What else should I know?"

"You should know about your powers. I think they're going to be quite strong, and so you mustn't do anything stupid."

I looked at her in disbelief. "Powers?"

She nodded impatiently, "Yes, your magic powers. You do realise you are a witch?"

## Chapter Two

I rolled my eyes. "Yeah, right, and monkeys might fly out of my butt."

"Don't be sarcastic, Emily, it encourages negative energy."

"OK, Iris, but seriously, I know you are into all...this," I waved my hand towards her fireplace, which doubled up as an altar, "but it's not my bag. I mean I like wearing black, it's better than this cat sick yellow they make us wear in school – sorry, Lyra, no offence," I apologised briefly to the cat, who licked her nose in response.

"But the black outfits aside, I don't really dig the image, and I don't want to be considered a freak at school, which I would be if I went around saying I was a witch!"

"Do you consider me a freak?" Iris asked as if it had genuinely never occurred to her.

I could hardly say yes, even though I wanted to. "Oh, ah, um," was the best I could come up with.

Mercifully she just laughed. "Thanks, Emily. Listen carefully: you are going to become a witch at midnight whether you want it or not. You don't have to tell anyone and you really don't have to wear black. But you do need to know what you're doing. Please, just humour me in this?"

"Humph, fine, I'm a witch." I said. "So, do I have some magical destiny to fulfil?"

She furrowed her brow, "No, why would you?"

"Well, I don't know," I spread my hands, "Isn't that normally how it works?"

"Not so far as I know. You just get your powers. It's up to you what you do with them. But you have to be careful; there are rules, of course, against openly using them."

"Right, yes, rules. Will the vampires rip my head off? Or the Ministry snap my wand or something?" I said, letting the sarcasm creep back in.

Iris sighed slightly but all she said was, "Your wand. Mustn't forget that." She went over to the Welsh dresser against the wall, and reaching right up to the highest shelf, she reverentially took down a small grey book and a stick.

Placing them on the table in front of me she wiped a tear from her eye.

"This is your sixteenth-birthday present from your mother. Her wand and her Grimoire."

"These were my mother's? She thought she was a witch as well?" I said it sort of jokingly, to cover my emotions. My mother left these for me? I choked back a tear of my own; I would think about that later. I ran my finger down the dusty cover of the grey book.

Iris put her hands on her hips. "She didn't just think it, Emily, she was an amazing kitchen witch."

"Kitchen witch?" I was lost now.

"Yes, she was particularly skilled at brewing. And your Grannie Mara is a fantastic hedge witch, so you have it from both sides."

This time I choked on a laugh of disbelief. "Oh, come on! You can't tell me that my father's mother is a witch too? My dad would bust a gut."

"Your father chooses to ignore the obvious all

too often," she said sadly. "Are you not aware of your grandmother's unusual herb garden?"

I looked at her in amazement. It was true my grandmother did grow all sorts of unusual plants, and on the rare occasions we visited her she would show her garden to me and try to teach me the names of the things.

I struggled to get my head around it all. Again I retreated into taking the mickey to move past something I wasn't ready to comprehend. I picked up the wand.

"It's a stick," I said flippantly.

"Yes," Iris said calmly, "in essence it is a stick. The wand has no actual power of its own, but it will give your magic some direction. The crystal in the end will enhance your magic too, making it stronger."

I looked at the end, and buried in the wood was indeed a small crystal. I waved the wand around.

"Expelli…something!" I intoned, then looked around expectantly.

Iris huffed; I think I was starting to annoy her.

"This isn't Harry Potter, Emily. And secondly, you don't actually have any magic, yet."

I put the stick down and picked up the book. "What's a Grimoire when it's at home?"

"It's basically an instruction manual. How to cast a circle, how to create magical objects like talismans and amulets, how to perform magical spells, charms and divination, and also how to summon or invoke supernatural entities."

I flipped through the pages, a little overcome as I saw it was filled with my mother's neat handwriting.

I wished she were here.

"OK, Aunt Iris. Thank you for these presents. Is there anything else I should know?" I wanted to go home now and look at my mother's book.

Iris stroked Lyra as she jumped onto her lap. "Oh, Em. There's so much you need to learn, but perhaps you've had enough for one night?"

I nodded.

She stood up. "The fact you inherited the craft from both sides is going to make you very powerful, do you understand? But until tomorrow we don't know exactly what your powers will be, so just be careful not to do anything stupid – and promise you'll call me if you have any questions?"

She then took off one of her necklaces and put it around my neck. "From Lyra and me, for protection. Happy Birthday, sweetie." She planted a kiss on my forehead and I gave her a hug, before collecting up my new belongings, stuffing them in my school bag and heading home.

That night I sat up late reading my mother's Grimoire. It was an amazing book and my mother had clearly taken all this witch stuff very seriously. How could I never have known? Why hadn't my father told me? I knew he liked to bury his head in the sand, but was I really a witch?

Inside the front cover of the book was a poem of sorts, entitled "The Witches Rede". It said:

*Bide the witch's law ye must*
*In perfect love and perfect trust*
*Eight words the Witches Rede fulfil:*
*An ye harm none, do what ye will.*
*What ye send forth comes back to thee*
*So ever mind the law of three*
*Follow this with mind and heart*
*Merry ye meet, and merry ye part*

I couldn't help but think it sounded more like something from "Pirates of the Caribbean" than a Witches Rede. But I took its meaning on board. Kind of a "do as you would be done by, or else" message.

I heard the church clock strike midnight and tensed, wondering if anything magical was going to happen. Would I be surrounded in a blaze of white light or float to the ceiling as I got my powers? I sat cross-legged on my bed and looked round; nothing was different.

I let out the breath I had been holding and rolled my eyes. *Of course* nothing was different; how silly to have let myself be sucked in to thinking it might be.

That's when I saw the ghost materialise in my chair.

## Chapter Three

I screamed, loudly.

Sitting on top of the clean laundry on my bedroom chair was an honest-to-goodness ghost. A boy of about my own age, but in a transparent grey. I kept screaming.

My door banged open and Duncan stood there in a t-shirt and boxer shorts. "What the bloody hell are you screaming about?" he demanded, rubbing his eyes sleepily. "I thought you were being murdered!"

"Ghost!" I whispered pointing at the chair.

The boy in the chair sat up, startled. "You can see me?"

"Yes, I can see you!" I didn't take my eyes off the ghost as I scrambled off the bed towards the reassuringly solid frame of Duncan. "Go away!"

Duncan looked at me like I was mad. "I guess you were having a nightmare? Don't worry, I'm going!"

"Not you." I clung to Duncan.

He looked extremely surprised. Normally I avoid being anywhere near him.

"Can't you see him?" I asked Duncan, digging my nails into his arm.

"It was a bad dream," Duncan said in a soothing voice, as though dealing with a child. "Go back to bed." He shook off my hand and slid out of the door before I could display any more unusual behaviour, shutting it behind him.

I made a move to open it and run after him, but the ghost held up his hands as if surrendering. "Please wait! I promise I won't hurt you."

I looked at him suspiciously.

"Please," he said again, "I've been here for years and no one has ever been able to see me."

"Here?" I was horrified. "In my bedroom?"

"Well, I can go anywhere in the house, but I like it in here best."

"You've been watching me all the time?" I was getting mad. "Like some kind of Peeping Tom?"

He had the audacity to smile. "Nothing else to

do. I like watching you."

I put my hands on my hips. "As in, when I'm getting changed?" I shuddered to think of all the things he might have seen. Somewhere in my anger at being spied on I had lost my fear of him.

"Yes," he confirmed cheerfully. Then, seeing my expression, he added, "I don't follow you into the bathroom though. I think you should have some privacy, and some things are best left unseen, don't you agree?"

"Oh, well, that's alright then!" I said furiously. "I suppose I should be grateful you have some limits, you bloody pervert!"

"Now, now, Emily. I'm only human. Well, sort of, anyway. You didn't know I was here; there was no harm in it. Spying on your parents is pretty dull, though sometimes I hang out with Duncan and watch him play computer games, but it's boring when you don't get a turn."

I sat back down on my bed. "How long have you been here? What happened to you? What's your name?"

"I'm Peter." He held out one hand as though to shake mine but I leaned back away from him.

"Ah, yes, right, can't shake anyway," he said, not in the least offended.

"How long have I been here?" He sat back down on my pile of clothes and tapped his lip thoughtfully. "Quite a while I think. For a long time before you came, anyway."

"What happened to you? You don't look very old to be, um, dead."

He couldn't have been more than sixteen himself, and actually he would be kind of handsome if he wasn't all grey and ghosty.

He smiled. "It's a great story. My whole family were butchered to death right here in this room. It was a bloodbath. We never found out how the killer got in, and they never caught him, he could still be around now. My four brothers are still here too, roaming around the house, spying on any naked girls they can find."

I put my hands over my mouth in horror, looking round the room for some signs of blood on the carpet or walls. "I feel sick." I genuinely thought I might throw up.

"I was just joking!" he said, seeing my white face.

"What? You sleaze rat! You scared the spit out of me. What really happened?"

"Well, it was early in the eighteen hundreds, and I was working as a chimney sweep. I was getting a bit big for the job and I got stuck in that chimney there." He nodded at the chimneybreast that ran from the living room up through the house. "My boss got me from a workhouse and was a cruel man. No one cared that I didn't come back out, in fact my bones are still just behind that wall."

I looked at the chimneybreast with concern but I didn't react quite as badly this time. "Are you serious? It sounds like something from a bad movie."

"Hmm, you got me, I think it is from a bad movie actually."

"Peter!" If he'd been solid I would have whacked

him.

"OK, OK, well, there was this great white shark…"

I folded my arms and glared at him.

He smiled ruefully. "Sorry, so much time on my own, I think I've gone a bit peculiar. The truth is that I don't remember. I don't remember anything much about my life at all. I know I've here since before television was invented. It totally brightened up my dull existence when I saw my first TV show. I love TV!"

He looked longingly at the small television in my room. "You couldn't put your 'Friends' DVD on for me, could you? The one where Phoebe teaches Joey to speak French? I love that episode, it's hysterical."

I groaned, but got up, flicked through the box set and inserted the requested DVD. I put the sound on low and climbed into bed. I was just plumping up the pillows behind my head to watch it better when Peter sidled onto the bed next to me.

I gave him a look, but moved over slightly so he

could lie next to me comfortably, though why I cared about the comfort of a ghost was beyond me; surely he could just sort of float?

One of my arms drifted downwards and went through his stomach. It felt cold, but nothing more. I pulled my arm back.

"Emily?"

"Yes, Peter?"

"How come you can see me now? You never could before."

My eyes snapped open wide. "Because it's gone midnight," I said, slowly letting it sink in. "And I'm now a witch."

"Oh, right." He seemed to accept that without question. Then he looked excited. "You could help me cross over! I seem to remember that only a priest or a witch can help a stuck spirit to the other side, is that right?"

"I don't know, sorry. I'm kind of new to all this. I'll ask my aunt tomorrow." I yawned and tried to focus on the show as my eyelids drifted closed.

Tap. Tap. Tap.

My eyes snapped open. It was daylight and I was in bed alone. I wondered if it had all been a dream after all, and then the tapping noise started again.

I glanced at the clock, feeling disorientated; it was already half past ten in the morning. I guess my father let me sleep in because it was Saturday.

I looked around for the source of the noise. A huge crow was standing on the sill right outside my window.

"Come on, witch, open up!" Surely the bird didn't just say that?

I approached the window tentatively. "Hello?" I said, feeling stupid.

The bird tipped his head to one side. "Hello," he answered quite distinctly, "any chance of opening the window – its bleeding freezing acorns out here."

I must be going mad, I thought. I considered shouting for my father. Aren't crows supposed to be evil? But this one could talk. Maybe it was some kind of rare parrot?

"Look, lady," the crow said, "I ain't got all day whilst you dither, I'm here on a matter of business."

I opened the window an inch. "What kind of business?" I said suspiciously.

"I'm 'ere as your new Familiar." He ducked his head to me, in what I guessed was a respectful gesture.

"My Familiar?" The word itself sounded, well, familiar. "Is this a witch thing?"

"Yes, ma'am. You've just come into your powers; I figure you don't have a Familiar yet?"

"Well, no." I cracked the window open a little more, still suspicious. "Who sent you?"

"No one sent me. I heard the gossip, of course. There's lots of gossip when a new witch gets her powers, and you're radiating power; all the animals can sense it." His beady eyes were fixed on mine.

"So let me get this straight," I tried to get my sleep-addled brain working; "you heard I needed a Familiar, and so you flew over here to offer your services?"

He bobbed his head. "The early bird catches the worm, if you'll excuse the pun."

"I see," I said thoughtfully, but I wasn't sure about it at all.

"You'll get a lot of cats applying for the position," he went on, "but I can be much more useful, take messages for you, spy without being noticed. I know owls are popular right now, but honest, gov, owls are useless, they sleep all day and keep you up all night asking for dead mice. I fend for myself and I'm house-trained too, I don't poop indoors."

"Um, good," I said, wondering if perhaps I was still dreaming. "So what's in it for you? Why would you want to be a Familiar? Wouldn't you rather just do what you like?"

"It's worth it, especially for a bird." He answered. "Gets me higher up the 'pecking order' if you'll excuse another pun. I'd be under a witch's protection. No one messes with a Familiar; I could even taunt the foxes."

If a bird could smile then I'd swear he was smiling at that idea.

I shook my head, trying to clear my brain. "How come I can hear you talking?" I narrowed my eyes on him.

"Because you're a witch now." He gave me a look that said "Duh!"

I mulled that over for a minute. "Why do I need a Familiar?"

"All witches have a Familiar!" He seemed shocked by the question, so I didn't pursue it. I figured I had a lot more reading to do if I wasn't going to look as thick as two short planks in this new world.

"What's your name?" I asked.

"Bob."

"*Bob?*"

"What's wrong with Bob?" He looked offended.

I felt bad for insulting him. "I guess I was expecting something more otherworldly," I said lamely.

"What, like Rumplestiltskin?" If a bird's eyes

could roll, this one's did. He grumbled quietly for a bit, then clarified, "It's short for Blackbobhead. But I prefer Bob."

"Yes, I can see why. Bob, thanks for stopping by and all that…"

"Listen, lady…"

That was the second time he'd referred to me as *lady*. "Don't call me that, it makes me sound old – I'm only fifteen. No, hang on, it's my birthday today, I'm sixteen!" I felt all giddy and happy to finally be sixteen.

"If you take me on then I would call you Mistress," Bob said.

"Really?" I sort of liked the sound of that.

He cocked his head, "Wanna give it a trial run? Just call when you need me. I've memorised the timbre of your voice now and we birds have an amazing sense of hearing."

"OK, Bob, you're on. Come in. Come and meet Casper, I mean Peter, he's my ghost." I had totally lost my grip on reality now.

"Peter?" I called, unable to see him anywhere.

His head appeared through the wall. "Oh, good, you're up. I got bored when the DVD finished, and I can't put on a new one. Could you put the next series in for me?" His body followed his head into the room.

"This isn't the time for watching TV," I said. "It's my birthday and it looks like I'm definitely a witch."

"A very powerful witch," Bob said proudly, "and born on Halloween too? A very powerful witch indeed."

"Yeah, but all that Halloween stuff is just nonsense, isn't it?" I said, suddenly not sure if it was or not.

Both Bob and Peter gasped at my ignorance. "It's All Hallows Eve!" Bob chided me. "The veil between this world and the next becomes very thin – a lot of spirits creep through, especially those that are invited, and they bring a lot of magic with them. The air literally hums with it. Everything you do on Halloween is more powerful, and being born on the 31st of October makes you doubly powerful. The planets line up in the same place they were at when you were born; don't you think that would have some effect? Not to mention that this particular Halloween is also a full moon. It's like a cosmic overload out there today."

"So, I'm like the witch version of 'The Omen'?" I felt really out of my depth.

"I don't know 'The Omen', Mistress, but I do know you need to be careful, today of all days, not to do anything stupid."

I sighed, "Why do people keep telling me that?" I had a feeling that maybe I should just spend the day in bed with the duvet over my head.

## Chapter Four

"I'm up now," I said more to myself than to my two strange companions. "Why don't you two take yourselves off so I can get dressed?"

Bob nodded obediently and flew out of the open window. I closed it behind him to keep out the October chill.

Peter settled himself back in my chair. "Don't mind me," he said, "I've seen you getting dressed hundreds of times."

"Yeah, well, I didn't know you were there then! The free porn is over." I went over to my chest of draws and started pulling out clothes.

"Wear the black lace undies, they're my favourite," he teased.

I collected a bundle of clothes, and added some huge grannie knickers to make a point, and said, "I'm going to change in the bathroom. If you even think of following me in there I will personally locate your bones and stomp on them, got it?"

He leaned back in the chair and laughed, but I figured he was smart enough not to push me.

Half an hour later I'd showered, dressed, and was fixing my makeup back in my bedroom.

"So I guess we should go and see my aunt?" I addressed Peter, who hadn't moved. "She might be able to give me some advice about helping you."

"I can't leave the house, remember?" Peter sighed.

"Oh, right, of course. I'll go see her and get back to you. I have a party to go to tonight so I need time to get ready for that. I'm going to have breakfast and then I'll go straight there. I should be back around four, is that OK?

Peter shrugged. "I've waited this long, I can wait a few hours."

Breakfast was great. Clare, my dad's girlfriend, had laid the table for a birthday brunch, with me at the head and several presents in front of my plate. She can be quite nice sometimes.

"Hello, Pumpkin." My dad put down his paper

and gave me a kiss. "Happy birthday." I think he calls me Pumpkin because I was born on Halloween.

They had all been waiting for me, and Clare went and made scrambled eggs with smoked salmon, which are my absolute favourites.

I opened my present from Duncan first; he'd got me all the Batman films in a box set, which was pretty cool, even though I suspected he just wanted to see them all again himself. I thought that Peter would probably enjoy them too.

Next I unwrapped one of the parcels from my dad and Clare. It was soft and black. I held it up. It was a floor-length black cloak, with fur trim and a velvet-lined hood. It was gorgeous, and just perfect for the party tonight.

"Thank you, I love it!" I gave my dad a hug, and even gave Clare a kiss on the cheek as she appeared with our food. She looked surprised and quite pleased.

I opened the others after we'd eaten and got a pretty good haul. Grannie Mara had sent me a book on the magical properties of plants, as well as fifty pounds. I wondered if she knew I would be getting my powers today.

Taking it all upstairs, I dumped it on my bed and then picked up my mother's wand and Grimoire before heading out to see Iris.

I entered the shop behind a guy and two girls. Lyra was sitting on the counter giving all the customers a once-over. She was looking at the three people in front of me.

"Dead-beat. Time-waster and possible thief. Really ugly skirt," I heard her say, commenting on each of them.

"Lyra!" I chided, really excited that I could hear her talking.

"Miss Emily." Lyra jumped down off the counter, looking flatteringly pleased to see me. She rubbed her face against my ankle. "I'll go and tell my Mistress you're here."

"Thank you." I said it quite quietly because the girl that Aunt Iris employs to help her on a Saturday was looking at us.

Iris came out of the stock room at the back, cleaning charcoal off her hands.

"Emily, how lovely. You haven't done anything, uh, unusual yet, have you?" Iris glanced at Jill, who was serving "ugly skirt".

"Not really. But I would like to talk to you. Are you very busy?"

"Fairly. Halloween is always my best day, plus I have an awful lot to do before my Coven meeting tonight. But I think your needs probably merit some special attention, so Jill will just have to cope." She raised her voice to Jill: "I'll be upstairs, just push the bell if you need me."

"Lyra said that one of those girls was a potential thief," I whispered as we went over to the stairs.

"Not a problem," Iris smiled. "There's a protection spell on the shop. If she tries to steal anything in her pocket or bag it jumps right out again before she gets to the door. Very embarrassing for the thief; they never try it twice."

Up in her flat, I noticed white powder along all

the windowsills, and even a line across the doorway. "What's that? Something magical?" I asked.

"Just regular salt," she said. "It keeps out the evil spirits, they can't cross a line of salt. And there will be a fair few of them out tonight. You should do the same at your house."

"Yeah, I can just imagine Clare's face if I put salt in all the windows!" I grimaced. "Speaking of spirits…" I filled her in on my encounter with Peter.

"Oh, that poor boy!" she said. "Do you have any idea what his unfinished business might be?"

I shook my head. "He doesn't seem to remember much about his own life. Not even his last name. I can't quite work out what his clothes are, some kind of suit I think, so it's hard to date when he died; but I think it might be quite a long time ago. He speaks as if he is modern-day, but he does like to watch TV, so he might have caught up." I shrugged. "If he died a long time ago then presumably anyone connected with his unfinished business would also be dead?"

"That is a problem." Iris tapped her foot whilst

she considered it. "It's quite a specialist subject. If only your mother were here; she was great with helping ghosts pass on."

"Really?" Another new bit of information about my mother, and perhaps another gift I might have inherited from her?

"Hmmm, but it takes a while to master—we really need someone who already knows what they are doing. I know!" She turned to me, excited, as a thought struck her. "You must come to my Coven meeting tonight. It would be a great chance for you to meet other witches, and I know they would all be thrilled to meet you too. There's a witch there, Theresa, who has some experience with spirits. Bring Peter with you."

"But he can't leave the house," I said, not at all enthusiastic about going to her Coven meeting.

"Can't you bind him to you instead of to the house? I'm sure the instructions will be in your mother's Grimoire. As I said, she did quite a bit of work with spirits."

I shrugged, "Maybe. But I have a party to go to tonight. Would it take long?"

She pulled a face at my selfishness. "I don't know, I'll ask Theresa for you. We meet at eight at The Seven Sisters; you should have plenty of time to get to your party as well."

The Seven Sisters were a famous group of beech trees on the town common near my house. It was right on the edge of town, so fairly private, but also fairly easy to get to. Planted hundreds of years ago, the trees were now incredibly tall, and stood in a large circle surrounded by open space. I could see how they would make a good place for a Coven to meet.

Despite several interruptions from the shop downstairs, Iris managed to teach me quite a lot over the next couple of hours.

I learned about casting a circle and about the four elements. It turns out my aunt is an Elemental Witch; her element is fire. I was excited about the idea of being able to control one of the elements, but after a lot of failure at trying to get a response from fire, earth, water and even the air, we had to conclude that I probably wasn't one of the elemental witches.

I couldn't imagine being a Kitchen Witch like my mother; my dad and I lived mainly on baked potatoes before Clare and Duncan moved in and Clare took over our meals. I could chop up a salad, no problems, but cooking was not my strong point. Only last month I had tried to microwave some eggs, but they had all exploded quite spectacularly; apparently you can't microwave eggs still in the shell.

I also seriously doubted I was a Hedge Witch, like my Grannie. Years ago I had tried to grow cress and mustard for a school project. I was the only person in the class whose seeds did absolutely nothing at all.

Iris patted me and said we would find my "metier", whatever that was. "You're probably an Eclectic Witch, Emily," she said, which confused me even more, "It means you have a bit of this and a bit of that, but hopefully a bit of everything you need. It would make sense."

We went thorough some of the spells in my mother's Grimoire. All the spells had to be said in rhyme, and some of them had to be said three times over, which seemed rather a faff.

We took a break for afternoon tea, and I slumped down on the sofa. I was starting to get frustrated. Apart from being able to hear animals talk and seeing a ghost, I had not actually managed to perform any magic at all so far.

I had waved my wand and said spells but nothing had happened. I had put ingredients in a cauldron and stirred it anticlockwise while chanting, but it could have been done by anyone; nothing magical occurred at all.

I could see Iris as well was beginning to wonder if I really had any magic. I felt a total idiot waving a wand, and like a total cliché stirring a cauldron. It was hardly inspiring.

"I think I'll go home," I told Iris. "I'm clearly not a risk as a witch. Less of the 'powerful' and more of the 'pathetic', I think."

Iris gave me a hug. "It will come, Emily. I don't think we've found where your talents lie, but I'm convinced you will have some. You *must* do." She said the last bit forcefully and I wondered if she were trying to convince herself as much as me.

"Try to *feel* it a bit more," was her last piece of advice as we went downstairs. "It's not a mental thing, magic must come from the heart."

As a birthday present, Iris said I could have any supplies I felt I needed from her shop, so I went round with a basket picking out the things that took my fancy. I stocked up on tall thin candles of all colours as well as some thick white pillar candles. I got some incense called Halloween, which had a lovely cinnamon smell, and a wicked-looking "ceremonial" knife called an Athame. I also selected a red velvet cushion, as a little present for Bob to sit on.

"Please think about coming to the Coven meeting," Iris said as she showed me out.

"Mmm, maybe," I said, deliberately not committing myself. There was no way I was missing the party for that.

When I got home the house was empty. I ran up to my room to get ready.

"Peter, are you in here?" I called. I got no response so I started to undress.

"Boo!" He popped out of my wardrobe.

"Aghh! You creep!" I was already down to my bra and knickers. "OUT!" I pointed at the door. He smirked at me and went through the wall instead.

## Chapter Five

I grumbled to myself as I pulled on my fancy-dress witch tights, but in truth I wasn't massively bothered; I was getting used to the idea that he'd seen it all already.

Ten minutes later I twirled in front of the mirror. I was wearing a sexy little black dress, the black and white striped tights, and some black pointed heels. I had a witch's hat ready and a broomstick for good measure.

The irony of my outfit struck me as hilarious. I'd bought it days ago, before I knew any of the inherited witch stuff. Now I almost wished I'd gone with the cat costume that had looked super sexy. Unfortunately I had decided that it was *too* sexy, it just wasn't me – I'm much more a kooky witch than a sex kitten. We are what we are, I giggled to myself.

"You can come back now." I raised my voice.

Peter floated back through the wall. He wolf-whistled at me, which I appreciated, so I struck a pose for him. "Very nice," he said approvingly. "So did your aunt have any advice on helping me cross over?" he asked, and I felt really selfish for making him wait.

"Sorry, Peter. She said it was pretty complicated. There's something in my mother's Grimoire but I haven't looked at it yet. She did say there was a witch in her Coven that might be able to help, though."

He nodded enthusiastically. "That's great. When can you see her?"

I groaned inwardly. I really didn't want to do this tonight of all nights, I wanted to go the party and see Sean.

"She'll be at The Seven Sisters for a Coven meeting tonight…" I said slowly, trying to think of a way out of it. "But let's look at the Grimoire first, maybe there is something I can do."

We both sat on my bed as I flicked through the pages.

"Here it is." I found two spells, one for banishing a ghost and one to help a willing ghost cross over.

"Oh damn. Ideally we need your bones." I was

grossed out at the idea of touching bones, even if Peter knew where to find them. I was certainly not going to dig up any dead bodies. "Oh, *or a ghost willing to stand inside a cast circle*; we have that! The tough bit, apparently, is that we have to connect, and it takes a powerful witch to do that." I paused, not keen on telling him that so far I was pretty much a bust as a witch.

I heaved a sigh. I would have to give it a go; it was that or tell him I would rather go to a party than help him cross over.

I looked at the clock; it was only six-thirty but it was already pitch dark outside. The autumn nights were really drawing in.

"We have some time. Let's give it a try," I said. "I'm only going to do a really simple circle, because I've never done anything like this on my own before, OK?" I got up and collected the white candles I had just been given by Iris.

I set four candles down in a large circle and turned off all the lights. My curtains were open and the room was now lit just by the full moon outside. I seated myself in the middle of the candles with a box of matches, some incense and an incense holder.

"You'd better come sit in here as well," I said to Peter. "Apparently, once the circle is cast you shouldn't be able to cross in or out. We mustn't swear in the circle, and if I leave it, it will break, so have we got everything?"

Peter nodded; he looked worried but he came and sat down beside me.

I opened the Grimoire in my lap and began to put into practice what I had learned from my aunt that day.

I tried to remember where the sun rose each day so I would know which way was East.

I began to recite: "Watchtower of the East, Guard and Bless this Circle." I lit the first candle. "Watchtower of the South, Guard and Bless this Circle." I lit the next candle and then repeated the words for West and North. When all four candles were flaming away, I lit the incense. I let the smoke follow me as I slowly turned round in a full circle and said, "As above and so below." Then I waved the incense a bit to make sure the circle was fully cleansed, before putting it in the incense holder.

I stifled the urge to giggle; I must have looked ridiculous, especially as I was wearing my full-on witch costume. I bit my lip and managed to get a more serious look on my face.

I seated myself opposite Peter in the middle and held out my hands palm-up.

"Do you think you could rest your palms on mine?" I asked him. He lightly put his ghostly hands over mine and I resisted a shiver as I felt him there.

"OK, this is the tough bit; we have to concentrate on each other, like a Vulcan mind-meld." I closed my eyes and tried to sense him without them. I was concentrating so hard I didn't hear anyone come into the house.

"Emily? What time are you planning to leave tonight?" It was Duncan's voice right outside my door. The doorknob turned and the door began to open.

"Don't come in!" I shrieked. I threw my hands out towards the door and there was a blast of yellow energy. The door, which was now half open, slammed shut again, knocking Duncan back through it and into the wall of the hallway. The candles flared up for a moment and then went out.

"Oh no!" I scrambled to my feet and opened my bedroom door. Duncan was sprawled out in the hallway completely unconscious, and there was a massive crack in the wall where he must have hit his head.

"What just happened?" I asked Peter desperately.

He shrugged. "Some pretty strong magic? Is it supposed to come out of your hands like that?"

I looked down at my hands, expecting some evidence of magic, but they looked normal. "I don't know, but I don't think so."

I slapped Duncan's cheek lightly, trying to get him to wake up, but he didn't react. I felt a bump on the back of his head and there was a matching red mark on his forehead where the door must have really whacked him.

"Help me drag him into my room, quickly, before the parents get back," I said over my shoulder.

Peter gave me a look and I remembered he couldn't touch anything. So I dragged Duncan by his ankles through my door; he weighed a ton.

"I need help! I'll be in so much trouble for this. They might not even let me go to the party."

I switched on the lights and scrabbled in my bag for my phone. I tried to ring Iris, but got no answer. I was starting to panic when inspiration hit me. I went over to the window, opened it and yelled, "Bob!"

He was there in seconds, a black shape appearing against the moon. I stood back and he flew in.

"Yes, Mistress?" He looked sleepy, and I wondered if birds went to bed as soon as it got dark.

"I need you to find my aunt and tell her I've knocked Duncan out. By *accident*," I added as Bob tipped his head at me questioningly. "I was casting a circle and he came into the room; I sort of blasted him."

"Blasted him, Mistress?"

"Yes," I held my hands up to Bob, "Like this, and some kind of burning light came out of my palms and hit the door and it knocked him out."

"You didn't say any kind of spell?" Bob looked intrigued.

"No, is that normal?" I already knew by the look on his face that it wasn't.

"Were you pointing your wand at him?" Bob seemed to be trying to comprehend what happened as much as I was.

"No. I already told you, it came out of my palms. Look, never mind that. Can you find Iris or not?"

"Yes, of course, Mistress, I'll be as quick as I can." He gave me one more speculative look and then flew out the window.

I went into the bathroom and ran a flannel under the tap, and then returned to my room and applied it to Duncan's forehead.

"Do you think I should ring an ambulance?" I

asked Peter.

"How will you explain it?" he asked sensibly. "He's only knocked out. I'm sure I saw a spell in your book, when we were looking through it earlier, to 'Revive' a person.

"Oh, great idea. Though I doubt I could make it work, let's have a look."

I retrieved my Grimoire from the circle.

"Yes! Here it is. Oh pants, it's pretty complicated. I need a load of stuff." I went round the room collecting what I had.

I had to run downstairs to get an apple, a glass of water and a bowl of some earth from the garden, but then I was ready.

I sat back down inside the candles and grimaced at Peter. "Wish me luck."

I cut the apple in half with my Athame on a mirror to double the strength of the spell, and reading from the Grimoire I said "I offer this apple to the Goddess and ask for the power of the full moon to fill me."

I removed one seed from the apple and, cradling it in my palm, I said "Seed of life, I give you air," then I blew on it. "Seed of life, I give you earth." I planted it in the bowl of earth. "Seed of life, I give you water." I watered the earth. "Seed of life, I give you fire from the father sun and light this candle to guide you." I lit a red candle and stood it in the earth. Then I picked up my wand, pointed it at Duncan and intoned:

"By earth, air, fire and water, let the power of the elements reside.

In perfect love and perfect trust, this man I want you to revive.

This is my will, hear my plea, as it harm none, so mote it be."

Once again nothing happened at all. I gave a wail and dropped my wand. Storming over to Duncan, I shook him hard. "Revive, Revive, Revive!" I sobbed in frustration.

This time the light burst out of me in like a ring around a planet, and then it slowly grew and grew, until – whoosh – it exploded outwards. Out of the window I could see the light fill the garden and beyond, and then everything went dark again.

My bedroom light flickered and then came on again.

Duncan sat up; the mark was gone from his forehead and he looked fine. I slumped in relief.

"Who the hell is that?" Duncan asked, looking over my shoulder.

I turned my head and gasped. Peter wasn't a ghost anymore. I'd "revived" him too. He was now a handsome sixteen-year-old boy, standing in my room, and that suit I had been unable to place? It was a pair of striped pyjamas.

## Chapter Six

I don't know which of us looked more shocked. All three of us were pretty stunned. Peter was pinching himself as if to check he wasn't dreaming, and I was gawping at him with my mouth open. Only Duncan looked confused rather than surprised.

"Um, this is Peter," I told Duncan, whilst trying to come up with a good excuse as to why there was a boy in my bedroom wearing only his pyjamas. Actually – forget a good excuse, any excuse at all would have done. I came up with … nothing!

Peter recovered quicker than I did. "Hi … Duncan, isn't it?" He gave Duncan a smile. "I know this looks really odd, but I had a massive row with my father last night; he got kind of aggressive and then he kicked me out of the house. Emily was nice enough to offer me her floor for the night. We're old friends and I just didn't know where else to go. I've been lying low because I don't want my dad to know where I am until he calms down, you know?"

Duncan nodded sympathetically. "Oh, right. Bummer."

I was taken aback by how easily he accepted the decidedly ropey story. But it did explain everything, even Peter's clothes. I supposed that Peter must have had a lot of time on his hands to think up his tall tales.

Peter kept his focus on Duncan. "Um, now that you know I'm here, I don't suppose I could borrow some clothes off you, could I? We're about the same size."

I never thought Duncan would do something as selfless as lend his clothes – I mean, he went mental once when I borrowed his coat just to bolt to the car and back in the rain to fetch my school bag. But he just nodded again and got up, slightly unsteadily, and left the room.

"I think he's got concussion," I muttered, looking at the door Duncan had just exited through. "He must have, to accept that story!"

Peter shook his head. "I knew he'd understand; after all, his own dad is the same."

"Huh?" I was confused. I knew Clare and Duncan didn't see his dad, but I'd never heard he was aggressive or anything.

Peter gave me a look. "I hear things hanging around this house. Duncan's had it pretty rough from his dad; maybe you should cut him some slack?"

I blinked a few times, realising that I had never asked or cared before. Maybe I should have.

"Whatever," I mumbled; "can we deal with the fact you appear to have come back from the dead?"

Peter's face lit up. "Yeah! You are one righteous witch, Emily Rand! Bringing back the dead. That's got to be major league magic."

"I don't know," I said, "I didn't mean to do it!"

We both jumped as Bob tapped his beak on the window. "Oh, thank heavens," I said, letting him in. "What did aunt Iris say?"

Bob gawked at Peter. "Holy hemlock," he chirped. He looked at me. "She's coming now, in her car. But you've got big problems, Mistress. I don't know what you've done, but there are a load of, uh, *dead bodies*, heading this way." He jerked his head at the window, and Peter and I rushed over to look out of it.

From the window I could see right down the hill to the common. It was really dark outside, but there was definitely something moving slowly over the common in this direction.

I felt sick. "What are they?" I whispered.

Bob looked worried. "For want of a better word, I would say 'Zombies'. They all bust out of their graves a few minutes ago. I assume you didn't call them on purpose?"

"No." I clutched my head, trying not to wet myself from fear. I mean, I've played "Resident Evil" on my PlayStation, and zombies are no laughing matter.

"Are you sure they're coming here?" Peter asked.

Bob nodded. "The spell came from here. I felt it. In fact, I saw it. Big yellow light? Pretty hard to miss. It went over the cemetery and then all these bodies started coming up. Only men, though, which is weird."

"The spell to revive." Peter looked at me. "You said 'this *man*' in the spell. It worked on me as well as Duncan; do you think it worked on all of them? There must be hundreds of dead men buried in this town."

"Just this town?" Bob said, really not helping my nausea. "How do we know how far the spell went?"

"What do we do?" I whispered. I slumped down to the floor, still unable to face looking at the zombies again.

"Another spell?" suggested Peter.

I wailed, "But I don't know what I'm doing! This is a nightmare!"

With his usual sense of crap timing, Duncan came back with some clothes for Peter. Bob dived under my bed to hide, and Peter and I looked at each other, both thinking the same thing: we had to get Duncan out of the way.

Duncan held out some clothes for Peter and said, "These should fit. Are you coming to the party tonight? Because if you are then I might have a spare costume if you wanted."

Despite the zombies on their way here, I took a second to wonder if Duncan had always been so friendly but I'd just never given him a chance.

Peter nodded and said, "That would be fantastic, can I come and look?" He practically pushed Duncan out of the door. On his way out he said under his breath, "Don't worry, I'm sure your aunt will know what to do."

Of course! Iris was coming, I ran back to the window. The zombies were at the bottom of the hill; they moved very slowly, so I figured I had a few minutes. Where was Iris? The whole road seemed deserted despite the fact it was now only about half past seven.

Then I saw her headlights. The zombies reached the road about the same time she did. Her car stopped for a second and then sped up exponentially and screeched up the hill.

"Keep an eye on them," I called to Bob as I ran downstairs to let her in.

"There's something very odd going on." She

sounded breathless. "Maybe it's just kids, but I swear I just saw grown men dressed as…"

"Dead people?" I asked, giving her a shaky smile.

"Oh my stars!" She slapped her forehead. "I knew it felt wrong. What have you done?"

I dragged her up to my room, shut the door and quickly explained.

"Wait a minute." She held up a hand. "Let's get this clear. You say energy came out of your hands?"

"Yes, and then out of my whole body when I did the Revive spell." I spoke fast, anxious about how much time we had before flesh-eating zombies tried to kill us. "Iris, can you do a spell, *quickly*?"

"No," she said calmly. "I don't have the power." Then she looked almost excited as she said, "But you do. I just knew you'd be special. Emily, you're a *Natural Witch*!"

I looked confused, obviously.

"OK, never mind right now." She stroked the crystal around her neck thoughtfully. "But it's a rare type of witch. You'll need some specialist training."

"Iris!" I almost shrieked at her. "I don't care. We're about to be attacked by the walking dead! What should we do?"

"Oh," She looked surprised. "They won't attack. You called them. They'll await your command."

"Are you serious?" I was giddy with relief.

She nodded and opened the window. "Tell them to wait in the garden, out of sight; we don't want them traipsing mud in the house."

I leaned out fearfully. An awful stench hit my nose. The first of the zombies was just entering the garden, hundreds more behind him.

"Uh, listen up, zombies." I called out nervously. "Could you all wait in the garden, or the neighbours' gardens? But stay out of sight, get off the road please."

I was thrilled and amazed as they blundered about trying to do exactly as I had instructed.

"What I don't understand," Iris frowned, "is how you managed to revive them too. Didn't you cast a circle before you did the spell? It should have been contained within it."

"Yes, I did, but…" my voice trailed off as I looked at the candles on the floor and remembered leaping across the room just after I knocked Duncan out. "I broke the circle," I finished lamely. "And I didn't recast it before I did the Revive spell." I hung my head.

"Why didn't Bob remind you?" Iris shot Bob an irritated glance.

"She didn't call me." Bob hunched his little shoulders and gave us both a cross look.

"Emily," Iris scolded me, "You must never do magic without your Familiar. He will act as your second pair of eyes, he will keep you grounded, and once you have bonded, his presence should add greatly to your magic."

"Well, I didn't know that. Sorry, Bob." I reached out and stroked his head with one finger.

"So without the circle, how far has the magic gone? Have I revived all the dead men everywhere? Or just all the dead in England, or what?" The thought sent shivers down my spine.

"Oh no, it's highly unlikely you've even covered the whole town. Definitely not beyond." She seemed confident and I sighed with relief.

"Well, that's something anyway." I looked out the window again. Zombies were still arriving, but there were apparently no more on their way.

Peter came back into the room; he was wearing a onesie with a skeleton motif on it. "It seemed appropriate." He laughed as I raised an eyebrow.

Iris coughed, trying to catch my attention subtly.

"It's OK," I told her, "Peter knows everything, he's my ghost."

"She revived me too." Peter explained as Iris registered disbelief.

"Oh dear," Iris sighed. "We have an awful lot to do tonight. Your spell only worked on Peter and the, uh, zombies, because it's Halloween. The veil between the living and the dead is very thin tonight, but come midnight the veil will drop down again and they will all return to the way they were."

I thought about that for a second. "But isn't that

good? The zombies will go back to being just dead bodies?"

"Yes, but in your garden! We have to get them back in their graves. And what about Peter? Tonight is the best night of the year to get him to cross over; he could be stuck here for another year whilst you learn what to do."

"Aw, really?" Peter said. "Do I have to go tonight? I was hoping to take the old body out for a spin. Get out of this damn house, maybe smooch a few ladies." He waggled his eyebrows at me.

"But then you would become a ghost again at midnight." Iris reiterated. "Do you want to stay here another year, until the veil is this thin again, to pass over?"

Peter shook his head. "I don't think so. No offence, Emily, but if I have to listen to your music for another year I'll go crazy."

"There's nothing wrong with my music," I huffed. Though I suppose I do have an unfortunate habit of singing along to musicals, which no one was ever supposed to hear!

Iris clapped her hands to get our attention. "We can try a reversal spell. I can write a spell, but Emily will need to provide the power."

"How do I do that?" I asked.

"What did you do before?" she said.

"I don't know! It just sort of happened."

Iris sighed, "Oh dear. This is the problem with Natural Witches. Your powers are attached to your emotions. You can't just invoke them with words, you have to do it with feelings."

"Well, that's easy then," I waved my hands at the window. "I definitely feel that I want the zombies to go away." I aimed my palms at the window. Nothing happened. I shook my hands like you might shake a faulty toy; still nothing. I blew a long breath of irritation out of my cheeks.

"It's not working." I stamped my foot in frustration and my bedroom light flickered again.

"You aren't focussed enough," Iris said, looking up at the light with concern. "I'll write the spell, it might help."

She pulled a pad off my shelf and a pen from beside it and began to write. "There," she said, handing it to me.

I read aloud from the paper:

"Undo what I have done,

Return the dead from where they come

In their graves undisturbed peacefully

This is my will, so mote it be."

"Try saying it three times," Iris suggested when still nothing happened; there was no bright light, and the zombies continued to moan quietly outside.

I did; we still had nothing.

"Right, that settles it," Iris said, "I'm taking you to my Coven meeting, right now. When a Coven adds their magic together it can get pretty powerful. You can use our magic to enhance your own."

"Yeah, OK." I should have known I would end up going. Too bad about the party, I thought, feeling defeated.

"I think you had better bind Peter to you before

we go, just in case." Iris nodded to Peter, who was flicking through one of my magazines.

"How do I do that?" I asked.

"I'm afraid the quickest and simplest method would be a blood binding. As Peter is currently corporeal it should be easy." Iris handed me a needle. "Both of you prick your fingers please."

We did. "So do we press them together?" I held my bleeding finger out towards Peter's.

"No, I'm afraid you have to ingest it. Suck the blood from his finger and vice versa."

"That's just revolting!" My stomach turned.

Peter was less bothered. He grabbed my finger and put it in his mouth, holding his own out to me. I gingerly sucked it.

Weirdly, the process felt quite erotic. My eyes caught and stuck with Peter's as we sucked at each other's fingers. I'd never noticed his eyes much before. They were a gorgeous blue-green. I felt myself suddenly incredibly drawn to him. Then there was a bang of light and we both staggered back, losing any physical contact.

Iris nodded in satisfaction. "Well done, Emily. A perfect binding."

## Chapter Seven

"We'll have to sneak out of the house," I said. "Otherwise, Duncan will think I'm going to the party without him."

The other two nodded, and we gathered up what we needed and snuck downstairs.

At the front door Peter paused. "This is kind of a big deal for me," he explained as I accidentally walked into his back. "The world has changed a lot."

I took his hand. "Not in this town it hasn't." I tried to reassure him. "We have a cinema complex and a bowling alley, but otherwise I don't think there has been any progress here since they installed street lamps."

He smiled at my lame attempt, and curled his fingers into mine.

My stomach flip-flopped a bit. I wondered if it was weird to feel that way? I suddenly didn't want him to leave.

All romantic thoughts flew from my head as I

stepped outside and the smell hit me.

It was full-on revolting. I pulled my cloak round to cover my mouth.

"Hey, zombies, please make your way to The Seven Sisters," I shouted through the material. Then, as I tugged on Peter's hand, we all dashed for Iris's car.

The dead smell was slightly sweetened by all the dried lavender, sage and rosemary she had in the car. She started the engine and drove quickly down the hill as the mass of zombies started to slowly follow.

It was just gone eight as we approached the clearing.

"Wait here" – Iris stopped Peter and me as we drew near – "I'll have to explain things first."

I nodded and slipped my hand back into Peter's, where it had become comfortable staying.

"Do you really want to go tonight if we can manage it?" I asked him.

He nodded sadly. "Yes, sorry, but apart from you I have nothing to stay for. You've got a life to live,

I've got an afterlife." His fingers stroked the back of my hand.

Bob dropped out of the sky and onto my shoulder. "They're ready for you now, Mistress."

We went forward. The circle of women parted and greeted us. I counted nine women, all dressed in black cloaks not dissimilar to my own, underneath which they were wearing... nothing at all.

Their ages ranged from about twenty to about sixty. I really wished they would stop flashing the flesh. I was so not cool with it.

They had big welcoming smiles on their faces for me, but were looking at Peter with rather unfriendly eyes. We held hands a little tighter.

Iris came forward. "This is Emily, and this is her ghost."

There was some muttering and then as if by silent agreement they all came and hugged us both. I tried not to shrink away from the wobbly bits coming too close.

The eldest woman took my hand; Peter had

dropped it to avoid one of the more cuddly witches. "Emily, if everything Iris says is true then you are a Natural Witch! We would be very glad to have you join us."

"Er, thanks." I muttered.

"Come, child, we will form a circle and draw down the moon." The other witches returned to the circle shape within the ring of trees as she spoke.

"Draw down the moon?" I thought briefly of the movie where someone lassos the moon. "I don't know how to do that."

"You don't need to do it, just stand in the centre with your ghost and we will do the rest. Just raise your arms up and try to feel her energy pouring down, around and into you." She walked me to the centre of the circle; Peter followed.

"We'll cast the circle and you will take the place of the priestess. Our power should generate in the circle and you will harness it."

"I will?" I looked around, feeling once again totally out of my depth. "Then what?"

"You'll know, dear," she said smiling; "after all, you're a Natural Witch. Now if you want to leave your clothes over there?" She pointed to a pile of clothes by a tree.

"Huh?" I stumbled backwards. "I'm not taking off my clothes!"

A small frown creased her forehead. "You need to feel the moonlight on your skin. It has to connect with your magic."

At that moment a moaning became apparent. The zombies had arrived. The other witches began to back away looking fearful.

"Zombies stop!" I said, feeling super important and powerful. The zombies stopped and stood swaying and moaning.

"Please hurry, dear," the eldest witch shooed me over to the tree, "this is all most unsettling and rather smelly. We really must resolve it and quickly!"

At the tree I found Iris shedding her clothes. "Quickly, Emily, get undressed; you can keep your cloak on for warmth." She disappeared back into the throng.

I looked at Peter; he had never left my side and was now trying very hard not to laugh at the look on my face.

"Oh, don't be such a prude, Emily, just get on with it. You have to do it or the zombies and I might be following you around for ever."

I huffed a little but began to undress. I supposed I had nothing he probably hadn't seen a million times before, but it was different now I knew him. I didn't want to get naked in front of all those women, but then I supposed they were all naked too. And what about the zombies, they were all men! A disgusting thought followed that one, that most of the zombies probably didn't have eyes anymore anyway.

"Turn your back at least!" I snapped. He gave into his laughter but turned around.

Once I was naked, I pulled my cloak tightly around myself. It was freezing.

Peter and I walked to the centre of the circle and the other witches began to chant. I didn't really listen to the words. I felt the energy and power instantaneously. It was as if it were bouncing around between the seven trees. The witches began to dance. I felt the chant as if it were music and I too began to dance without conscious thought. The energy began swirling like a vortex with me in the eye of the storm. I threw my arms up to the full moon and let it wash over me.

I heard Bob's voice somewhere above me. "Now, Mistress."

"Undo, undo, undo," I cried.

The moonlight shot into me and radiated back out of me. I was blinded by the glare and then it was dark again.

In the silence I dropped my arms. As my eyes readjusted to the darkness I could see the witches were all stood looking at me with awe. My gaze swivelled to the common around us. Not a zombie in sight. And there in front of me was Peter, once more all ghosty.

Ghosty and naked!

At his feet lay the onesie he had been wearing. It had dropped right off his ghost body. I remembered that his pyjamas were still at the house.

I tipped my head back and gave in to a hysterical mix of crying and laughter.

When I had calmed down a little I wiped my eyes and focused on Peter. He was glaring at me, with his hands over his manhood.

"You know what they say," I giggled, "revenge is a dish best served cold, and naked."

"Emily!" His eyes darted to the other witches, who were also starting to giggle.

I shrugged. "I don't know what to do now," I told him.

"I do." A pretty girl in her mid-twenties came forward.

"Are you Theresa?" I asked.

She nodded. "Here, take my hand and hold the other out to Peter. He's bound to you, right?"

"Yes." Peter rested his hand over mine as we had tried once before. I felt the bond straightaway; we were still connected.

"Good." Theresa smiled with approval, "That's the hardest bit. Now just imagine him surrounded by white light and repeat after me.

"Halloween moon, blessed night,

surround this man with cleansing light,

whatever keeps him, set it free,

release his bonds, so mote it be."

I repeated her spell three times. Peter and I stared into each other's eyes as I said the words, trying to convey everything we wanted to say, but really there wasn't much, only that in the last few hours he had become special and I would miss him. As I said the verse a final time, he mouthed "goodbye", smiled and glowed, and then he was gone.

"Goodbye," I whispered, "rest in peace."

Just like that, I felt the bond fade, and suddenly I was freezing cold on a dark autumn night, feeling lonely and overwhelmed.

As if sensing my need, Bob flew down and landed on my shoulder. I stroked his little head. "Let's get out of here," he said quietly.

I quickly got dressed and then thanked the witches one by one. Iris came up to me last of all. "I suppose you'd like me to take you to your party now?" she said, giving me a quick hug. I could see she was really proud of my performance.

"Yes, please." I had no idea how I was supposed to act in this situation, but I couldn't wait to get back to my normal life, where I knew exactly what I wanted. "But would you mind if we went and picked up Duncan first? I wouldn't want him to think I went to the party without him."

She looked at me in surprise, but I didn't explain. I was going to be much nicer to Duncan from now on.

Fifteen minutes later Iris dropped Duncan and me off at Tamsin's house. I could hear the song "I Put a Spell on You" blaring out from inside, and there were cut-out ghosts and witches in the windows.

Duncan made a decent vampire in his costume. I wondered about setting him up with Kate, she was such a "Twilight" fan.

As the door opened I thought I would feel sick with nerves wondering if Sean was going to be there and if he would talk to me, but after everything I had been through in the last day, I felt surprisingly confident.

I quickly found Bryony and Kate. Bryony was flirting with a boy I recognised as one of Sean's friends. Kate was standing to one side looking a bit left out. I hugged them both.

"Where have you been all day?" Kate asked, "I've been ringing your phone but it was always switched off."

"Sorry," I apologised, "just some family stuff I had to sort out."

"Is everything alright now?"

"Yes." I smiled.

"Hey, Kate, do you think you could chat to Duncan for a bit? I don't see any of his friends here yet."

"Sure," she smiled coyly at Duncan. He looked

delighted and a bit star struck at the sight of her in her "'Buffy" outfit. How had I never noticed before that they might like each other?

I soon spotted Sean chilling in the kitchen. He was dressed as a zombie. I laughed when I saw his costume. He looked absolutely nothing like the zombies I had accidentally raised. Much better-looking, for a start. I walked over.

He leaned over and kissed me on the cheek. He smelled a million times better than my zombies as well.

"I was starting to worry you weren't coming," he said, flashing lovely white teeth at me.

"I wouldn't have missed this party for anything," I said, knowing full well now that it was the truth.

He tilted his head, eyeing me appraisingly. "You seem different somehow."

I laughed again. "Do I?"

But he was right, I did feel different. I *was* different. For a start, the old me would never have approached him; I would have waited for him to come to me, and then I would have been really edgy and under-confident. Not any more.

He offered me a glass of "eyeball" fruit punch. I sipped it, smiling at him and listening to him talk. I didn't add much, just watched the way he ran his fingers through his hair, the way he was focused only on me.

Then I watched him and his friends do the full dance to Michael Jackson's "Thriller", and clapped appreciatively.

Eventually we moved out to a bench in the garden, only able to see each other by the light of the moon and the flickering of several candles that stood inside carved pumpkins.

It wasn't the most romantic song in the world, but he leaned in to kiss me as the "Ghostbusters" theme tune started in the house, filtering out of the living room window.

It was funny how the lyrics made me feel powerful. I was a ghost buster, in a friendly nice way. I was a "righteous witch", as Peter had said.

Instead of ducking my head, or turning away in fear at the last second, as I might have done before, I was ready for this moment.

Under a Halloween full moon, Sean Carrey kissed me, and I kissed him back.

I had earned this moment. Who knew what the future would hold, what other talking animals I would encounter, what ghosts I might have to help, what other spells I would cast that would cause complete mayhem, and whether my magic would be a major part of my life or just another element of who I was?

None of that mattered as I experienced my first real kiss.

This was one Halloween I would never forget.

*The End*

# Werewolf Magic & Mayhem
# (Book Two)

*So there I was, trying to think of some new way to tap into my powers, when a boy walked into the shop and I got a witchy tingle…*

New witch Emily Rand and her crow Familiar, Bob, are back for a full length bout of magical mayhem. Emily is approached by a handsome werewolf called Fletcher who wants her to cure him of his *affliction*. Despite her lack of experience, Emily decides to try to help Fletcher. Unfortunately her spells aren't known for going according to plan, and Emily accidentally divides Fletch from his human body and brings forth his inner wolf in a very real sense. Now she has to find a way to put it right by the next full moon or Fletcher will be stuck as a wolf forever.

*Keep reading for a preview of Werewolf Magic & Mayhem*

## Solstice Magic & Mayhem
## (Book Three)

It's the Summer Solstice and it's a full moon too. Natural Witch Emily Rand has been doing her best to keep her distance from gorgeous Werewolf Aaron Fletcher, but fate has other plans. Fletch's new pack Alpha has heard rumours of Emily's powers and is coming for her. He wants to bond his wolf to her witch and make himself the most powerful Werewolf in Britain. Can Emily and Fletch combine forces to outsmart the Alpha before the Solstice magic takes away their choice? Emily has never had great control over her powers and being forced into a battle to stop the Alpha can only result in complete mayhem as Emily accidentally sets spells in motion that she has no idea how to stop.

## Books by Stella Wilkinson

The Flirting Games
More Flirting Games
Further Flirting Games
The Flirting Games Trilogy
Good @ Games
Flirting with Friends

Halloween Magic & Mayhem
Werewolf Magic & Mayhem
Solstice Magic & Mayhem

Romancing the Stove
Bend it like a Bookworm
Game, Set, and Mismatch

Notice Me
A Christmas Gift
All Hallows EVE

# Werewolf Magic & Mayhem

## Chapter One

"Emily? Can you bring out some more green tallow candles and some dousing sticks, and get those Athames out of the bucket of water by the back door?" my aunt Iris called to me as I pottered about her stock room.

"No problem." I shouted back, doing as she asked. "Why were these knives in water outside?" I asked her as I carried them into her shop.

"I was imbuing them with the power of a *waxing moon* overnight," she answered, like that would make any sense to me.

The whole conversation would have sounded bizarre out of context. But Iris runs a shop full of paraphernalia for witches.

I've been a real witch for nearly three weeks now, and I'm still totally useless at it! I got my "powers" on my sixteenth birthday on Halloween, but apparently I'm a Natural Witch, which means my power comes from my emotions, over which I seem to have very little control.

So far I've managed all of five spells. After a disastrous false start I eventually managed to do a *Revive* Spell, but unfortunately also raised an army of dead zombies by accident, and corporealized a ghost at the same time.

I did, however, get right the spell to "bond" with my ghost *and* I managed to help him cross over.

I'm also proud to say that I very successfully managed to *Undo* my *Revive* Spell, which I count as another spell.

All that happened on Halloween, and what have I done since then? One spell, that's it! Not for the want of trying. My aunt Iris, who is a witch as well, has been trying very hard to help me "harness" my powers, but I can tell she's getting a bit depressed with how slow I am.

My one other spell since then was to bond with my Familiar. I have this cute crow who turned up on my sixteenth birthday and offered his services.

Now that I'm a witch, I can hear animals talking, which is one of the most exciting things to happen.

Bob, short for Blackbobhead, wanted to be a witch's Familiar because apparently they get a lot of respect from other animals, but it seemed like a bum deal to me because now he was constantly at my beck and call. Not that I've had much use for him so far. But he's taken to hanging out in my room. It's mid-November and pretty cold outside, so I can appreciate that it's nice to have a warm place to go if you're a bird. Also I tend to spoil him a lot; I bought him a red velvet cushion to sit on and I get him little treats. Not worms or anything gross, but he seems to have a weakness for Cheddar cheese.

Apparently having your Familiar present when doing magic can really enhance a witch's powers, but first you have to "bond".

The bonding process is kind of icky. We had to swap blood. Not just swap it but actually drink it fresh from each other. There are other ways to bond but blood bonding is the most powerful kind of bond, and

I need all the help I can get.

Bob was very sweet about it; I used my ceremonial knife, an Athame, and he let me cut him at the end of his wing bone (it's tough to find a feather-free spot on a crow) and he was fine about drinking from me. That was an experience I don't ever want to repeat. I had to gouge a hole in my palm that was ridiculously big and deep to allow his beak to suck from it. I had to wear a bandage round my hand for a week afterwards (and I didn't tell Bob, but I totally doused it in TCP as well, to avoid infection. I shudder to think where that beak might have been). Anyway, he sucked my blood and I almost puked having to suck blood out of his bleeding wing. Then as we did it we were supposed to have a "meeting of minds". This is the really difficult bit. You stare into each other's eyes until you connect.

I stared at Bob and tried to feel as one with him. It took only seconds, but as I sucked his blood it felt like it took ages.

It was actually an amazing moment; I got some weird sense of the pleasure of flying. I literally felt the wind beneath my wings, and the call of the open sky, then that all got muddled up with the scent of warm fresh earth, of wet rain, and then of sucking up worms and pecking in the dirt; then *bang*! A bright light went off between us and we were bonded.

Bob was pretty rude about the "mind meld". He said I thought about clothes, make-up and boys too much and that I was a "shallow human". But hey! I'm a sixteen-year-old girl, that's what I'm supposed to think about. Stupid bird.

I was incredibly pleased at pulling off the bonding. And relieved I wouldn't have to do it again any time soon. The taste of his blood was utterly disgusting. I would make a rotten vampire.

But that is the sum total of spells I've done. It's pathetic. I'm supposed to be a powerful witch, but can I do any basic magic? No.

Iris is a Fire Witch; that's one of the Elemental witches. She tried to teach me her own power, starting with the simple: how to call a flame. But after three hours of blowing on candles and matches, which made me incredibly light-headed, we had to conclude I didn't have it in me.

Since then I have tried to do all kinds of stuff. Mainly spells from the Grimoire I inherited from my mother. They were mostly potions, or supposed to be, but they came out looking more like pond water. My mother was a Kitchen Witch, but she died when I was five, so I didn't know until I got my own powers.

Aunt Iris is my mother's sister. She said I wasn't allowed to know until the day before I turned sixteen because "children" can't keep secrets, and so it's forbidden to tell them they are witches until just before they get their powers. There seem to be some silly rules.

For example, I'm not allowed to tell my friends I'm a witch. Not unless they too are witches, or some other magical being. At first I thought this was dumb, but I'm beginning to see the sense of it now.

People would want us to do spells for them if they actually believed it was real. If they *didn't* believe it, then we would be mocked as nutters, or worse, they might believe it and want to burn us! There were a lot of good reasons to be careful, no matter how far society has come since the famous witch trials.

I can just imagine my best friends' reactions. Kate would think it was cool and ask me to do some magic, which I would totally fail to do, then she would think I was making it all up. Bryony would say it was *satanic*. That's what she already thinks of my aunt's shop.

My aunt owns a shop called The Crystal Fire. It sells all kinds of witch stuff. People think she is just a Wicca worshiper; they don't know she can do real magic.

Since her usual Saturday girl left a couple of weeks ago, she gave me the job, and now I work from eight until six every Saturday for minimum wage. But I think of the job less as work and more as training. I'm familiarising myself with her stock and trying to learn what everything does. A lot of it is just "trash for the tourists" as Iris says, but some of it is actually quite powerful, if used properly.

So here I was, working the shop floor, trying to

think of some new way to tap into my powers, when a boy walked in and I got a witchy tingle…

## Chapter Two

I do already have a boyfriend. Well, sort of. Okay, not really.

I have a boy I like, and I think he likes me. We've kissed and been on a group date. Does that count as a boyfriend? I wish I knew.

I haven't updated my Facebook status, just in case.

The "not quite my boyfriend" boy in question is called Sean Carrey. He goes to the other school in our small town and I met him in our main shopping centre.

On Halloween we met up again at a party and we kissed. It was my first real kiss and I wasn't disappointed. Sean is quite a catch in my opinion. He is confident, funny and really good-looking, though I suspect he knows it, if you know what I mean.

So, Halloween went pretty well for me (after I had gotten rid of the zombies and the ghost), and Sean asked for my number at the end of the night.

This was a first for me as well, and I spent some

time screaming quietly down the phone to my girlfriends the next morning.

I had to wait a few days for his call; actually he didn't call at all, he texted me. His friend had asked my friend to go bowling and did we want to double?

It wasn't the most romantic way of being asked out but it was the best offer I'd ever had. The only problem was that Bryony, Kate and I had always done everything together, and now only Bryony and I were invited.

I made Bryony ring Matt, Sean's friend, and check it was okay if Kate came with us and brought a date, like a triple date, or a group date. Bryony is much more assertive than me, and she didn't remotely care about doing something that might put Matt off her. I would have been really nervous about trying to change the arrangements, but she just rang him up and told him how it was going to be! I am so in awe of that.

Finding Kate a date was easy. I have a sort-of stepbrother, who I think likes her.

My dad's girlfriend Clare moved into our house a

couple of years ago and she brought her son with her. I hated them both at first; it had just been my dad and me for years, but I was getting used to them now. Clare's son, Duncan, is the same age as me and now also goes to my school. I feel bad that I was so mean to him at first, and probably alienated him when he didn't know anyone, so I'm trying to be really nice now to make up for it.

After all, a witch has to consider her actions carefully. It's in the Witches' Rede; there's a line in it that goes: *What ye send forth comes back to thee, so ever mind the law of three.* I think it means that whatever magic I do will come back on me three times over, so I will be steering well clear of doing anything bad.

Though so far my spells haven't always gone according to plan, at least they were done with good intentions.

Anyway, I asked Duncan to come along as well and he jumped at it. The trouble was, his mother is quite protective, and insisted on dropping us off and picking us up.

Most of the date was pretty good, in my opinion. Sean and I teased each other over our bowling skills, and we held hands under the table when it wasn't our turn. But at the end of the night our hoped-for goodnight kiss was totally thwarted.

We all went outside to wait for our parents, and in the darkness of the parking lot, I noticed Matt start kissing Bryony. I was sure that Sean was leaning in for a kiss when my dad pulled up ten minutes early and started flashing his headlights at us.

There was no way I was going to kiss a boy with my dad watching!

In the end I just mumbled goodnight and shook his hand. It was so embarrassing. He said he'd call me, but I thought I might have blown it.

He actually did call me a few days later, and we talked on the phone for a while. So I'm pretty sure he still likes me. But he didn't suggest another date. Mostly we just talked about movies and food, and then suddenly he had to go, as his mum was calling.

Bryony keeps telling me to chill out about it, and

that boys are useless. But if he liked me as much as I like him, then wouldn't he want to see me as much as possible?

All of that leads me to the present moment. I was sensing this other boy, really *sensing* him.

It wasn't particularly his looks. He was definitely handsome, in a dark moody sort of way, but he wasn't as classically good-looking as Sean. Yet there was something *more* about him somehow. Like an old soul trapped in a young body. He couldn't have been more than seventeen, but he had "presence".

He was looking at the books in a dark corner of the shop, but even with his back to me I felt like he was looking at me.

The tingles up and down my spine were unusual. I was convinced it must be a witch alarm of some sort; I had never experienced it before.

I watched the boy move about the shop. Other customers moved out of his way, almost unaware that they were doing so. He didn't look directly at me, yet I continued to feel as if he was observing me somehow.

He took a book off the shelf and leafed through it, then for no reason he suddenly put it back and walked out the door.

"Well, that was weird." I murmured to myself. I went over to the bookshelf and picked out the book he had been looking out. It seemed fairly innocent; it was called *Magical Trees in the Forests of Britain*.

It was bizarre, but as I pressed my palm against the cover, I could swear I picked up a residue of his touch.

The trouble was that the feeling could easily have come off the book itself. There were so many titles in the shop that contained a bit more than the average book, and that sometimes left a whisper of power.

This particular book didn't look very powerful though. It was mainly for "Druids" who use trees as conduits, and harvest certain berries like mistletoe, for their brand of magic.

I put it back and told myself I was just being silly.

I was exhausted by the time six o'clock came around. I needed a long bath and to put some peppermint foot-rub on my tired feet. Iris paid me, which always cheers me up, and I helped with some last-minute straightening up before saying my goodbyes and leaving.

It was already dark and I felt strangely on edge as I began the short walk home.

Crossing the main road, I walked past the park, and there, sitting on a bench, was the boy from the shop.

I was sure he was waiting for me. I could tell he was looking at me.

I was instantly unnerved. Once again I could *feel* him more than I could see him. For a moment I considered breaking into a run. I was alone by a dark park and I was being watched.

Then I remembered: I didn't have to be alone!

I was still far enough away from the boy that with luck he would not hear me. In a low voice I called "Bob?"

Bob was supposed to come whenever I called. He had amazing hearing and was always listening for me, but now that we were bonded he should have been detecting my stress anyway. If he didn't come I could always yell for him; that would do it.

It might seem a bit lame having only a crow for backup, but if you've ever watched Hitchcock's "The Birds", you would know crows can be pretty scary when they want to, plus he could always fly to my Aunt Iris for a bit more "firepower" if necessary. As another witch she could also hear animals talking, though to any other person it just sounded like bird noises.

The boy looked upwards towards the sky at the sound of my voice. Could he hear me? Did he know I was calling a bird?

Bob came from the direction of my house like a black arrow, and I relaxed as soon as I saw him.

"Mistress?" he said, dropping onto my shoulder.

"Sorry, Bob," I lightly stroked his wing, "I just needed the company."

He put his head to one side, "I'm here whenever you need me, Mistress. Is something botherin' you?"

"Some*one*. I'm probably being stupid, but see that

boy over there? He's giving me the creeps."

Bob looked at the boy. "He is *different*." I felt Bob's claws tighten slightly on my shoulder.

"Different how?" I said, slowing my steps, not wanting to get too close yet.

"Dunno." Bob stared at him thoughtfully.

The boy stood up. "Emily." His voice was smooth. "I didn't mean to give you the creeps, I just need your help."

I stopped walking. How embarrassing! He had heard me even from that distance.

Wait – he'd said my name?

He began to move towards me, and I held my hands out protectively. I didn't think I would be able to do any magic without a spell, but I hoped that somehow my powers would protect me if I were scared enough.

"Who are you? How do you know my name?"

"I've been watching you for a while." He stopped walking to give me time.

"Oh, right, and that's not creepy?" My voice rose

an octave. "You've been watching me? Why?"

"Because you're a powerful witch. You are, aren't you?" He seemed unsure.

"Who said so?" I asked, taking another step back.

"I heard the animals on Halloween, they were all talking about you. It was you, wasn't it?"

"What are you?" I asked suspiciously, "Are you a witch?"

He shook his head. "Look, do you think we could talk properly? I don't really want to shout about it in the street."

"I'm not going anywhere with you!" I said in disbelief. "You've just admitted you've been stalking me."

Now I came to think about it, I had been getting this unnerving feeling of being followed for days now. I'd dismissed it, but now I knew it was real.

I heard him sigh. "I'm not suggesting dragging you off into the woods. Can I take you for a cup of coffee or something?" He nodded his head back up the street I had just come down; there was a coffee house at the far end.

I looked back up the street. It was much lighter at the other end; some shops were still open and I could see the odd person milling about.

"I've got a boyfriend." I don't know why I said that, but I blurted it out without thinking.

I could feel him smiling at me. "It's just a coffee, but extras *are* optional."

## Chapter Three

Was I being teased by a dark handsome stranger? Or was I being teased by a psycho nutcase?

"Bob?" I looked at the bird for his opinion.

Bob shrugged his wings. "He smells wrong, but not exactly evil. I'll stay with you."

"You can't come into a coffee shop, they'd freak out," I told him.

"What did the bird say?" the boy asked.

I looked at him with suspicion again. "I thought you said you could hear animals?"

He scuffed his foot impatiently. "Not all the time. It's complicated. Can't we just go somewhere and talk properly? Do you want to sit in the park maybe?"

"No way! The coffee shop is fine," I told him; then turning my head to Bob I said, "Will you stay nearby though?"

"Yes, Mistress; be cautious," he warned, then he flew up on to the nearest rooftop.

"Come on then, *stalker*. Do you have a name?"

He came nearer and reached out to shake my hand. "It's Fletcher; my friends call me Fletch."

"Hello, Fletcher." I stressed his longer name to show we weren't friends yet, and shook his hand.

Our hands connected and I got an electric shock. I pulled my hand back with a yelp. "What the frack was that?"

He gave a low chuckle. "It's an early warning system. It only happens the first time we touch. It's how one paranormal knows another straight off."

"Huh?" I'd never heard this. "I've touched other witches and that never happened," I accused him.

"It won't with your own kind." He said it like I was being dumb and that it should have been obvious.

"Ah-ha, what about with a ghost though? I touched a ghost and I didn't feel it!" I thought maybe I had caught him out.

"Ghosts can't be touched. Not really." He sounded tired of the topic and so I didn't pursue it. But I was getting a bit fed up with feeling like everyone else knew all the rules except me. I really had to learn more, and soon.

We walked to the coffee shop in silence. I thought about all the things Fletcher had said so far. I had a lot of questions, but I figured they could wait until we were comfortable. At least I had plenty of time. I'd told my father I might stay at Iris' for dinner, so no one would miss me for a while.

We got into the coffee shop and he asked what I wanted. Since he was buying, I asked for a hot chocolate with marshmallows, and then took a seat by the window where Bob would be able to see me. Fletcher went up to the counter, and in the light I was finally able to get a good look at him. He was taller than me, and had wide shoulders and a narrow waist. He looked like he worked out, and he moved gracefully. His hair was a thick rich dark brown; it was a bit longer than the usual fashion and kind of messy in style. I wondered if he used a product to achieve that "bed head" look. He was dressed all in black and his trousers were tight around his bum, hugging his legs, falling over heavyweight army-style boots.

He turned to look at me and caught me looking at his behind. I quickly turned my head before I could meet his amused gaze, but that didn't stop me from sensing his silent laugh.

Why was I ogling him? I already had a sort-of boyfriend! I didn't need another one, especially one I didn't as yet trust at all.

He put the hot chocolate down in front of me and took a seat opposite me.

I looked up, still slightly embarrassed, and was stopped dead by his eyes. I hadn't seen them clearly in the dark outside, but they were green. Not just a bit green, but brilliant green.

"So what are you?" I asked again.

He looked around to check no one could overhear us. "Werewolf," he finally answered.

"No way! Werewolves are real?" Why doesn't Iris tell me these things? That's a big one as far as I'm concerned. "How about vampires, goblins, pixies and elves?" That only touched the surface of all the mythical creatures I could think of.

He frowned at me. "You are a witch, aren't you? The one they were talking about? Or are you something else?"

"Yes, it's me – at least, I don't know if I'm the one you heard about. But I am a witch. I'm just a bit new to all this stuff..." I trailed off lamely.

"I was in wolf form on Halloween, it was a full moon." He stirred his coffee. "I can hear the other animals when I'm that way, but not as a human. They were all talking about a new witch who was especially powerful and could do some things other witches can't."

I was flattered, but still unsure that they were talking about me. "I don't know if I'm all that powerful," I confessed. "I've not really been able to tap into my powers very easily."

Fletcher was silent for a moment, considering. "Did you raise the dead?" he asked at last.

"Well, yes, but it was an accident." I was a bit embarrassed by that.

"I was there. I followed the rumours; I saw the

witches gathering and the dead dudes following your command. But I was in wolf form; my vision is different, and though I tried to memorise your smell, everything was overcome by the stink of grave."

I wrinkled my nose. I could remember only too well how rank my zombies had been. Another thought occurred to me.

"Oh my god, you didn't see me naked, did you?" How mortifying!

He gave me a "wouldn't you like to know" eyebrow twitch, which clearly indicated that he had.

"You said your vision was different?" I fished, hoping to glean some indication that this very handsome boy had not seen everything.

"Yes, that's true. I see colours and shapes rather than specifics. But I can confirm I wasn't just looking at your face." He laughed silently again as he drank from his cup.

I decided he hadn't really seen anything; after all, he hadn't been sure it was me at all. But he was flirting with me. Some flirting was definitely acceptable, however.

I blushed a bit, but I liked the way he talked to me; not many boys had given me that kind of attention before.

Then I wondered if he had an ulterior motive.

"So why have you been watching me?" I asked, dropping my smile.

He stirred his almost empty cup again. Like he was trying to work out what to say. In a low voice he began, "I was attacked by a werewolf two years ago. Apparently most don't survive the turn, but I did. It was extremely frightening and every single full moon is still terrifying for me. I'm afraid the wolf inside me is taking over. I'm worried about the safety of my family, and I don't want to be this way."

"I'm so sorry. I didn't ask to be a witch either, but I'm adjusting."

"It isn't the same. I lose myself when I turn. Not completely, but the wolf is stronger than me. Sometimes I feel him during the rest of the month, it's… unsettling." He still focused on his cup. "I found others of my kind. They aren't like me, they embrace the wolf. They said I should do the same, that I would be more comfortable in time. But it's been two years and I'm still terrified every month. I tried to stay away from my family. I tried to get far away at the full moon, but there isn't anywhere to go in this stupidly small country where you can keep totally away from people. I've had to leave home. I just can't risk being near them. I've got a younger sister and I don't know how to keep her safe anymore, safe from me!"

"So werewolves really do kill people? I've never heard of anything in the news." I didn't realise there were werewolves running around England; it was a scary thought.

"Actually they don't, on the whole. Apparently if you embrace the wolf, you become one with it and you can control its instincts. The one that attacked me had gone mad. He had fought the wolf and lost himself. I think that's happening to me."

My eyes widened with horror. I *was* having hot chocolate with a potential killer, after all.

"So why come to me? What is it you expect me to do?"

"I've been reading all these old books about werewolves, and there was a documented account in one about how a witch separated the man from the wolf. I want you to do it for me before the next full moon."

"You want me to cast a spell to separate you from the wolf inside you?" I clarified.

He nodded. "It takes a natural witch, which is what you are, right? I can't find any indication of another one anywhere, and I only have a week left until the wolf takes over again."

Oh brother! My spells so far weren't exactly known for going according to plan…

## About the Author

Stella Wilkinson is a full time author with fourteen books currently available, plus several multi-author anthologies. She is from Bristol, in the South West of England, UK, where she lives in a world populated mainly by her characters and where best friends, boys, flirting, kissing and the occasional paranormal creature are what she thinks and writes about. Although she is best known for her hugely successful Flirting Games Series, she also has two stand alone novels, several short stories, a middle grade sweet romance series, and another series titled Magic & Mayhem, which are romantic comedies about a disastrous witch, her crow and a certain werewolf. She also compiled and edited three anthologies for a children's hospital charity, which feature over seventy authors, including Stella, who all contributed short stories to the collection.

Stella is an enthusiastic (if dreadful) cook, and loves to bake chocolate brownies by the dozen. She also collects antique books and first-editions of any genre at all, so her walls are filled with dusty smelly old books on various boring subjects that she treasures and her family hates :-)

She hopes you enjoy the books and looks forward to catching up any time you feel like emailing her through her website. Also check the website for details of upcoming new releases!

www.stellawilkinson.com